D0542485

This is the story of how Mike and Sulley met. You can read along with me in your book. You will know it's time to turn the page when you hear this sound....

Let's begin now.

NARRATOR: TINO INSANA
MIKE WAZOWSKI: BILLY CRYSTAL
JAMES "SULLEY" SULLIVAN: JOHN GOODMAN
PROFESSOR KNIGHT: ALFRED MOLINA
DEAN HARDSCRABBLE: HELEN MIRREN
ART: CHARLIE DAY
SQUISHY: PETER SOHN
GREEK COUNCIL PRESIDENT: AUBREY PLAZA
KID #5: MARLEY PEARSON

PRODUCERS: TED KRYCZKO AND JEFF SHERIDAN

Walt Disney RECORDS PIXAR ANIMATION STUDIOS

First published by Parragon in 2013
Parragon
Chartist House
15–17 Trim Street
Bath BA1 1HA, UK

Printed in China

Disney · PIXAR
MONSTERS
UNIVERSITY
MU
Parragon
Bath • New York • Singapore • Hong Kong • Cologne • Delhi
Melbourne • Amsterdam • Johannesburg • Shenzhen

When Mike Wazowski was little, he decided to be a Scarer when he grew up. He studied hard and finally he got into Monsters University. He was thrilled.

"I can't believe it ... I'm officially a college student!"

On the first day of class, a monster named James P. Sullivan showed up. Everyone called him Sulley. “Roooooar!” Sulley was a natural talent.

The teacher gave him a wide smile. “I expect big things from you.”

Sulley didn't think he needed to do any studying.

Mike thought Sulley was lazy. "I'm going to scare circles around you this year."

"Okay, I'd like to see that."

Mike studied hard all semester and his teachers noticed.

"The answer is C, 'Fangs'!"

"Well done, Mr. Wazowski!"

At the final exam, Mike and Sulley got into a fight. They destroyed a special scream can!

Professor Hardscrabble, the Dean of the School of Scaring, was furious. "You will not be continuing in the Scaring Programme."

Mike and Sulley were crushed. Now they'd never be Scarers! But then Mike remembered the Scare Games. He and Sulley got Hardscrabble to agree to a deal.

"If you win, I will let your entire team into the Scare Programme. But if you lose, you will leave Monsters University."

Mike and Sulley's team was a fraternity called Oozma Kappa. Its members were not scary at all.

Sulley couldn't believe it when he met them. "Are you kidding me?"

But Mike thought he could teach them to be scary.

The first challenge in the Scare Games was a complete disaster. Mike and Sulley rushed ahead, leaving the rest of the team behind. Oozma Kappa was almost eliminated.

A fraternity named Roar Omega Roar won.

Mike gathered Oozma Kappa. "I will tell you exactly what to do and how to do it." He thought it was the only way to win.

Sulley decided he wasn't going to train with them. He waved goodbye to Mike. "You tell them what to do, but not me."

The next challenge was the 'Avoid the Parent' event. Oozma Kappa practised a lot, except for Sulley.

Mike coached the team. "Slow."

But Sulley was impatient. "Faster!" He hurried ahead and almost got caught!

Squishy, one of the misfits in Oozma Kappa, surprised everyone. He had gotten the flag in the challenge without anyone knowing. He had saved the day!

The other monsters were excited. "We did it!"

Team Oozma Kappa was doing better, but they still didn't think they had what it took to be scary. Mike took them to Monsters, Inc. to see the Scarers. "See what they all have in common?"

"No, not really." Everyone looked puzzled.

"Exactly." Mike smiled. "There's no *one* type of Scarer."

After that, they were a real team. Even Sulley joined in the training. Mike pushed them hard. "Scary feet! Scary feet! Scary feet!"

Team Oozma Kappa made it through the 'Don't Scare the Teen' event and they stayed hidden in the 'Hide and Sneak' event as well. Soon it was announced that there were only two teams left.

"We're down to two remaining teams: Roar Omega Roar and Oozma Kappa!"

For the first time, Sulley believed they could win the Scare Games. He believed in Mike.

Then Dean Hardscrabble pointed at Mike and said something that upset Sulley. "Do you think he's scary?"

Sulley was worried. He decided to give Mike a little coaching of his own. "Just reach deep down and let the scary out. ROARRR!!"

Mike did his best, but Sulley was nervous. Maybe Mike just wasn't scary.

The final event took place in a scare simulator. Mike went last. Oozma Kappa was tied with Roar Omega Roar. It was all up to Mike.

Sulley looked him square in the eye. "Just go out there and show them what Mike Wazowski can do."

Mike took a deep breath. Then he went into the simulator and performed his most terrifying scare. "ROARRR!!!"

Sulley grabbed Mike when he came out. "We're in the Scare Programme!"

Oozma Kappa had won the Scare Games!

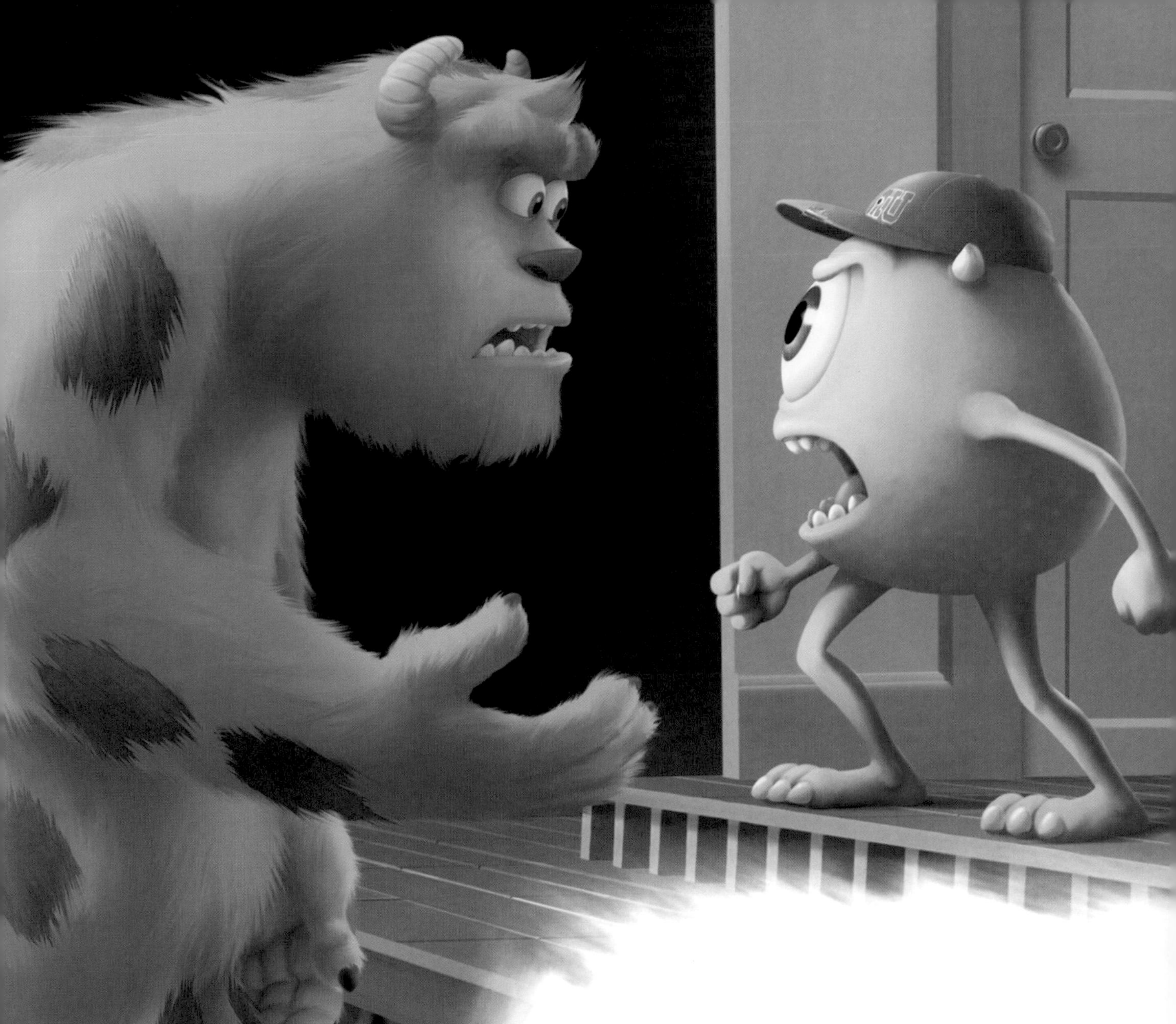

But Mike made a terrible discovery. Someone had changed the settings on the scare simulator so he would win.

Mike stared at Sulley. "Did you do this?"

"Mike … "

"You said you believed in me." Mike was heartbroken.

Mike ran off. Sulley felt terrible. He found Dean Hardscrabble and confessed.

"You did what?"

"My team had nothing to do with it. It was all me. I cheated."

Mike decided to find a real human child. He had to make it scream to prove he was scary.

Mike activated a door and stepped through. He was in a human child's bedroom!

He snuck up to the bed. "ROARRR!"

The child looked at him and then smiled. "You look funny."

Mike soon realized he wasn't in a bedroom with one child. He was in a summer-camp cabin with many children. Like any monster, he knew children were very dangerous. He was toast!

Dean Hardscrabble acted fast. She had the door to the camp closed.

But the Oozma Kappa gang distracted the guards and Sulley barrelled through.

"Sullivan! Don't go in there." Hardscrabble was concerned.

Sulley found Mike near a lake by the cabin. The camp rangers hadn't seen either of them.

"You were right." Mike stared out at the lake. "They weren't scared of me."

Sulley sighed. "Mike, I'll never know how you feel, but you're not the only 'failure' here."

Mike was surprised. He realized Sulley was his friend. He agreed to go back to the monster world.

But the door had been deactivated. That meant they couldn't return!

Mike came up with a plan. "This could work!"

He and Sulley decided to scare the rangers.

After clawing the floor, slamming the door and overturning beds, Sulley roared loudly. "ROARRR!!"

The rangers were so frightened, their screams were the loudest ever!

The power from the screams made the door open. Mike and Sulley went back to monster world. They were in big trouble.

Hardscrabble kicked them out of Monsters University but let the rest of the team stay.

Sulley looked at Mike as they left. “So, what now?”

Mike wasn’t sure. “I don’t really have a plan.” But it wasn’t long before Wazowski and Sullivan were together again....

Mike and Sulley soon got jobs in the mail room at Monsters, Inc.

Mike was thrilled. "The team of Wazowski and Sullivan are going to change the world starting today."

And before too long, that's just what they did.